SUPERPOOP
NEEDS A NUMBER TWO

THIS BOOK BELONGS TO:

_____

_____

SAM HARPER · CHRIS JEVONS

FOR BIGGIE, FATIMA AND NOA
S.H.

FOR TOBY
C.J.

HODDER CHILDREN'S BOOKS
First published in Great Britain in 2023 by Hodder & Stoughton
1 3 5 7 9 10 8 6 4 2
© Hodder & Stoughton Limited, 2023
Illustrated by Chris Jevons

ISBN 978 1 44496 413 4

Printed and bound in China

Hodder Children's Books
An imprint of Hachette Children's Group
Part of Hodder & Stoughton Limited
Carmelite House, 50 Victoria Embankment
London, EC4Y 0DZ
An Hachette UK Company
www.hachette.co.uk
www.hachettechildrens.co.uk

SUPERPOOP
NEEDS A NUMBER TWO

Hodder
Children's
Books

Meet Superpoop - your friendly local **POOPERHERO!**

Since he joined the League of Superheroes, Superpoop's been
FLUSHING OUT the bad guys single-handedly.

But the **TOILET TROUBLE** keeps piling up.
Superpoop doesn't even have time for a **POO BREAK** . . .

Who's that at the door?

SUPERHERO
HQ
(SUPER-TOP-SECRET)

It's Mayor McGill!

"I have a very important job for you, Superpoop. The museum has a new treasure - a priceless ancient Egyptian **GOLDEN TOILET BRUSH.** We need to step up sewer security around the building."

"Here's a **SUPER-TOP-SECRET** map of the city's drains.
I know I can count on **POO!**"

Superpoop can't handle this **BIG JOB** all by himself.

"I need a **NUMBER TWO** to join my team!"

POOPERHERO TRY-OUTS

Uh-oh. Looks like no one
wants to do the **DIRTY WORK.**

But wait . . . what's that fresh fragrance?

"It's me! I'm WONDA WYPE

- your number one fan!"

"A toilet roll?!" laughs Superpoop. "You're too squeaky clean for drain work."

"Don't underestimate me," says Wonda.
"I'm fresh AND strong. I clean up messes like no one else!"

Superpoop remembers when all he wanted was a chance . . .

"Oh alright then . . . but you're going to need some **TOILET TRAINING,**" he says.

"Welcome to **POOPERHERO BUTTCAMP!**" Superpoop shouts.

"CHALLENGE ONE: THE PARP TEST!"

Can Wonda Wype handle the stink?

Yes! She's **TOOT**-ally smell-proof!

"Time to bring out the big guns," says Superpoop.

STINKY CHEESE

PARP!

Wonda Wype breezes through!

"Amazing!" says Superpoop. "How did you do it?"

"My flowery fragrance is strong enough to block any whiff!" Wonda explains.

"Time for
**CHALLENGE TWO:
THE FLUSH TEST!**"

Can she resist the
power of the jets?

Wonda Wype has a tight
grip, but Superpoop's turning up
the power! She's about to get
FLUSHED OUT when . . .

WHOOSH! Wonda Wipe ducks and dives. She jumps and dodges.
POW! She throws herself **HIGH** and . . . she sticks the landing.

"I've never seen anything like it!" says Superpoop.

Just as Superpoop is about to announce the final challenge . . .

"Oh no! The **POOP SIGNAL!**"

DEAR SUPERPOOP,

THANKS FOR LEAVING THE TOP-SECRET SEWER MAP
UNGUARDED, YOU SILLY PLOP! I'M GONNA BLOCK
THE DRAINS AND FLUSH THE GOLDEN TOILET
BRUSH OUT OF THE MUSEUM AND BECOME RICH!

MWAHAHAHAHAAAAA!

YOURS SNEAKILY,

SNAKEFACE

Superpoop leaps to action!

"I'm coming with you," Wonda cries.

"This isn't a test, Wonda Wype, and you're not
ready for the real deal. You'll only distract me!"

And without a backward glance,
Superpoop flushes himself.

"PLOPS AWAAAAAAY!"

"STOP, SNAKEFACE! Your plan is foiled!"

Superpoop tracks down Snakeface underneath the museum.

"Not this time, Superpoop," cackles the sneaky snake. "I only need one more poop to secure my blockage . . . and you're just the right size!"

Looks like Superpoop has **SKIDDED** right into Snakeface's trap. But then . . .

Wonda Wype SWOOPS in from above. SWOOSH!

She takes Snakeface by surprise
- POW!

She pulls Superpoop free
- YOINK!

And together they take down Snakeface as a team - BAM!

"Thanks for saving me, Wonda. I'm sorry I doubted you. Will you be my **NUMBER TWO?**" asks Superpoop.

"I'd be happy **POO!**" smiles Wonda Wype.

If you're ever in trouble,

call this unstoppable

POOPERHERO team . . .

. . . there isn't a mess that they can't **CLEAN UP** together.

"PLOPS AWAY!"
"IT'S TIME FOR A WYPE-OUT!"